Ten Little Squirrels

An old counting rhyme adapted by

Bill Martin Jr
and Michael Sampson

Illustrated by Nathalie Beauvois

BROWN BOOKS KIDS

Ten Little Squirrels

Brown Books Kids
Dallas / New York
www.BrownBooksKids.com
(972) 381-0009

A New Era in Publishing®

Distributed in New Zealand and Australia by David Bateman Ltd.

Publisher's Cataloging-In-Publication Data

Names: Martin, Bill, 1916-2004, author. | Sampson, Michael R., author. | Beauvois, Nathalie
(Illustrator), author."
Title: Ten little squirrels / an old counting rhyme adapted by Bill Martin Jr. and Michael
Sampson ; illustrated by Nathalie Beauvois."
Description: Dallas ; New York : Brown Books Kids, [2022] | Audience: Ages 4-8, grades 2-3. |
Summary: Ten little squirrels brainstorm a way to evade their natural foe until one of them sneezes. No need to get
squirrely--practicing classic rhythm and rhyme while teaching children to count has never been more fun! ""Ten Little
Squirrels"" by New York Times bestselling authors Bill Martin Jr and Michael Samson follows the ""tail"" of these furry
friends as they determine what to do when a dog approaches their tree. Readers can enjoy the charming illustrations,
count each of the colorful squirrels, and go nuts rereading to their hearts' content.--Publisher.
Identifiers: ISBN: 978-1-61254-600-1 | LCCN: 2022937403
Subjects: LCSH: Squirrels--Juvenile fiction. | Dogs--Juvenile fiction. | Counting--Juvenile fiction. |
Stories in rhyme. | CYAC: Squirrels--Fiction. | Dogs--Fiction. | Counting. | Stories in rhyme.
| LCGFT: Nursery rhymes. | BISAC: JUVENILE FICTION/Animals/Squirrels. | JUVENILE FICTION/Poetry.
Classification: LCC: PZ8.3.M418 T46 2022 | DDC: [E]--dc23

This book has been officially leveled by using the
F&P Text Level Gradient™ Leveling System.

ISBN 978-1-61254-600-1
LCCN 2022937403

Printed in China
10 9 8 7 6 5 4 3 2 1

For more information or to contact the author, please go to
www.MichaelSampson.com.

MS—To Valentina Sampson

NB—To my dog Luli

Ten little squirrels

played by a tree.

The second one said,

"A man with a dog."

The third one said,

The fourth one said,

"No, let's hide in the shade."

The fifth one said,

"I'm not afraid."

The sixth one said,

The seventh one said,

"They're looking all around."

The eighth one said,

"Let's run to our nest."

The ninth one said,

"No, staying here is best."

Then the tenth one sneezed . . .

Ker Ker Ker

KERCH

"Bowwow!" barked the dog.

"Time for some fun!"

And TEN little squirrels,

off they did run!

Squirrel Facts

Squirrels are very fast runners and run in zigzag patterns to escape predators.

Do you think it's possible for a dog to catch a squirrel?

The squirrel family includes ground squirrels, tree squirrels, and flying squirrels.

Have you ever seen a flying squirrel?

Squirrels work hard collecting and hiding nuts so they will have food for winter.

How do you think squirrels find nuts they have stored when the ground is covered by snow?

Squirrels are part of the rodent family and are related to chipmunks.

What's your favorite rodent?

Squirrels love to eat nuts, fruits, veggies, and even insects.

Do you think it's a good idea to feed wild squirrels?

Squirrels come in many colors, including red, gray, black, white, and yellow.

What is your favorite-colored squirrel in this book?

Squirrels live on every continent except for Australia and Antarctica.

Do squirrels live near you?

Squirrels can live for more than ten years.

Can you tell an old squirrel from a young squirrel by looking at them?

Squirrels are considered wildlife, and it's illegal to keep one as a pet.

Do you think a squirrel would be a good pet?

Squirrels have large bushy tails because it helps them balance.

Did you know that squirrels also use their tails to show they are happy, like dogs do?